Aya

MW00954272

Aya

Hanna Hymans Ostroff

Illustrations by Felicia Hoshino

H2Ostorybooks

San Francisco, California

Copyright © 2016 Hanna Hymans Ostroff

All rights reserved. No part of this book may be reproduced or transmitted in any form or by any means, electronic or mechanical, including photocopying, recording, or by any information storage and retrieval systems, except in brief extracts for the purpose of review, without the written permission of the author.

This edition published 2016 by
H2Ostorybooks
www.H2Ostorybooks.com

Library of Congress Control Number:
2012914121

ISBN: 978-0-9972642-2-7

Author: Hanna Hymans Ostroff, www.H2Ostorybooks.com
Illustrator: Felicia Hoshino, www.felishino.com
Designer: Jim Shubin, www.BookAlchemist.net

For my beautiful husband Greg
and our beautiful children
Zachary, Isabel, Samuel, Luc,
"Itadakimasu"
　　　　—H. H. O.

For Yoshi, Sora & Yume
　　　　—F. H.

May you live a beautiful life

and may you be peaceful.

Aya noticed beauty everywhere.

"Here to touch, here to see,

beauty all around me," she said...

when a hungry feeling
reminded her it was
time for breakfast!

Quick as a cat she climbed the branches.

Aya noticed something in the distance.

"A faraway view, I will travel to see it.
That's what I'll do!"

Walking through her
forest home, Aya noticed
beautiful things.

"Flock of golden birds,

murmur from a stream,

morning colors paint a sky
awakened from a dream."

It had been a long walk. Her stomach was empty.

Aya could see more steps than she could count and thought,
"I might be little, but I've never felt small.
Should I climb this staircase? It is beautiful after all."

She began to climb.

At the top, she pushed open the heavy door.

Inside, she noticed a small gathering.

Sitting together, they reminded her of
the golden birds she often saw in her home.

Chanting in a murmur,
they reminded her of the stream
running through her home in the forest.

Wearing robes the colors of sunrise,
they reminded her of home.

"I'm not quite sure why I've traveled here."

"If I do as they do, it might become clear."

She tried to sit still.

Her mind was not quiet and neither was her stomach!

Noticing a kind face Aya thought,

"She seems very nice."

"I do like her smile."

"But, why should I sit every day in that style?

Instead, I can spend all my time eating food
and searching for beauty
when I'm in the mood!"

The kind face spoke,
"Quietly,
sit with me and we can breathe peacefully.
While sitting still, I breathe and pray.
Peace unfolds in this quiet way."

Aya replied,
"Before I do anything,
without sounding rude,
I really must feed my stomach some food!"

After eating, Aya wanted to go home
but remembered the kind face and thought,

"How kind to share vegetables and rice!
Perhaps, I should follow her wise advice."

The encouraging smiles helped Aya to
practice how to sit quietly,

be still,

and ignore her hunger pangs!

Aya practiced sitting.
Aya practiced breathing peacefully.
In her stillness, Aya noticed something beautiful.

Aya was ready to return home.

The nuns noticed her absence.

They wondered where she had gone.

On the first day they thought,
"May she be peaceful."

On the second day they thought,
"May she be happy."

On the third day they decided to visit her.

Down
  many
    steps
      they
        walked.

They noticed the sunrise as their robes
brushed against the forest floor.

The murmur of the stream
reminded them of the
sound of their chanting.

In the snow, they found Aya sitting quietly.

When she opened her eyes,
Aya saw they were sitting quietly, too.

"All I need is near."

Aya touched her heart.

"My peaceful place is here."

Aya began to
climb the nearest tree.
She noticed her beautiful
friends smiling at her
and stopped suddenly.

With a quiet bow,
Aya thanked them
and for a moment
she was still.

Quick as a cat,
Aya continued climbing.
Time for breakfast!

About the author

Hanna Hymans Ostroff
enjoys short inspired quotes. Some of her favorites are "Yield to the present", "All because two people fell in love....family" and "Love is my religion." Rev. Hanna is an interfaith minister, officiant and writer living in Northern California.

www.H2Ostorybooks.com

About the illustrator

Felicia Hoshino
is a celebrated illustrator, living in San Francisco. Aya is her 6th children's book.

www.felishino.com

CPSIA information can be obtained
at www.ICGtesting.com
Printed in the USA
LVHW072343040719
623228LV00013B/139/P

9 780997 264227